Press

TO NICOLE
WITH LOVE

CASEY WEST

Artesian Press

P.O. Box 355, Buena Park, CA 90621

Take Ten Books
Romance

Other Take Ten Themes:

Mystery
Sports
Adventure
Chillers
Thrillers
Disaster
Horror
Fantasy

Project Editor: Dwayne Epstein
Assistant Editor: Molly Mraz
Illustrations: Fujiko
Graphic Design: Tony Amaro
©2003 Artesian Press

www.artesianpress.com

 Artesian **Press** ISBN 1-58659-188-6

CONTENTS

Chapter 1

The bell on Mr. Johnson's pet shop door jingled as Nicole stepped in. Mr. Johnson smiled and waved at her.

"Hi, Nicole. Come on over." He moved out from behind the counter. "How was school today?"

Nicole shrugged. "Okay, I guess."

"Well, good." He smiled. "Ready to learn about the shop?"

Nicole nodded.

"Well, I'll show you the birdcages first," Mr. Johnson said. "Then we'll head over to the puppies." He walked toward the back of the shop. Nicole followed him where a dozen birdcages hung from the ceiling in a row.

"These cages need to be cleaned a

few times a day," Mr. Johnson said. He pointed toward a cluttered corner. "There's a sink over there and fresh food on that shelf," he said.

"Sounds good," Nicole said.

The door of the shop jingled and a boy entered. Nicole recognized him from school. He walked behind the counter and threw his backpack on a shelf. He grabbed an apron and a scrub brush and began to clean one of the fish tanks.

"Oh, good," Mr. Johnson said. "I want you to meet Sam." He led Nicole over to where the boy was up to his elbows in fish-tank slime.

"Sam, this is Nicole," Mr. Johnson said. "She'll be working here after school now, too." Nicole looked up to see Sam smile at her.

"Hi," the boy said. He held out his hand.

"Nice to meet you," said Nicole. She looked at the slimy, wet hand and wasn't sure what to do.

"Oh, sorry," Sam said. "We can shake hands later."

Mr. Johnson began to talk again. "I was just about to show Nicole the . . ."

The phone behind the register rang.

"Sam, can you show Nicole how to clean the puppy cages?" Mr. Johnson picked up the phone. "Johnson's Pets," he said into the phone.

Sam turned to Nicole. "Right this way," he said. He winked and walked toward the front of the store. Nicole followed him.

Sam led her to the cages in the front window where a bunch of puppies slept in the afternoon sun.

"We just need to fill the water and food dishes and keep replacing the newspaper every few hours," he said. "These puppies sure do pee a lot."

Nicole frowned.

Sam laughed and opened a squeaky cupboard door next to the cage. "The food and stuff is in here."

"Okay, thanks," said Nicole. She bit her fingernail.

"So, do you always talk so much the first time you meet a person?" Sam grinned and grabbed a box of dog food from the cupboard. He dumped a pile into one of the bowls.

"Sorry, I'm just kind of shy, I guess," Nicole answered.

"I don't mind shyness," he said looking at her. He draped his arm over the side of the cage. "You go to Eastbrook High, right?"

"Yeah, I think I've seen you before," Nicole said. "This is your first year, right?"

"Yeah," he said. "My dad and I moved here this summer. So what brings you to the Animal Kingdom?" He grinned.

"I just . . ." She sighed and looked down at the ground. "Actually, my mom just lost her job, and there hasn't

8

been much money lately."

"Oh, sorry." He looked at his feet and then up at her. "Well, that's really cool of you."

"Thanks." She smiled and pet one of the puppies. "I love puppies. I've always wanted one."

"Now's the perfect time to buy one," he said. His voice sounded like a TV commercial.

She laughed. "I don't really have the money now," she said.

"Well," Sam said. He shut the cupboard and turned to face her again. "I guess I'll show you how to scrape the slime off the fish tanks." He grinned. "It'll be hard to share that job. I really enjoy it."

Nicole laughed. "I'll bet," she said. Nicole followed Sam into the storeroom.

Chapter 2

Nicole turned over onto her stomach. She held the telephone to her ear with one hand and picked lint off her bedspread with the other. She was talking to Grace, her best friend.

"So, how was it?" Grace asked.

"Okay." Nicole paused. "There's this guy Sam who works there, too. He goes to our school."

"Is he cute?"

"*What*?" Nicole asked.

Grace sighed. "*Cute*, Nicole. You know, when you think a boy is attractive and you would maybe like to go on a date with him."

"He was nice," Nicole said. "I think we'll be friends."

"You *do* think he's cute," Grace said. "I can tell."

"Okay, forget it." Nicole rolled over onto her back again and stared at the ceiling. Grace continued with her personal questions.

"Look, I just don't see why you are so shy with guys all the time," she said. "You never let yourself have fun. Take that guy Toby for instance. You know he really likes you, and you run for cover every time you see him."

"Not true," said Nicole. "I finally met him yesterday."

"What?"

"He was next to me in the cafeteria line," said Nicole. "He started talking about how much fat is in the mystery meat."

Grace snorted. "What did you do?"

"I was nice. I let him talk until it was my turn to pay, and then I said good-bye and sat down. What else could I do?"

"He*llo*!" Grace said. "Did you flirt with him at all?"

Nicole could tell Grace was annoyed, but she didn't care. She was not going to tell Grace she flirted when she didn't. "There was absolutely no flirting," she said. "Don't you get it?"

"I just want you to enjoy high school," said Grace.

"I know, but I just don't want to be one of those girls always flirting with every guy at school. It's just not how I am, and . . ." Nicole stopped. She didn't want to start a fight with her only real friend.

"All right, all right. I get the message," said Grace. "But one day, you will have to go on a date."

"Yeah, maybe in college," Nicole said. She closed the window blinds and turned her lamp on. It was getting dark outside.

"That's in three years, Nicole." Grace sounded shocked.

Nicole rolled her eyes again. "I was kidding," she said.

"Ha ha, very funny," Grace said.

"Look, I need to finish my algebra," said Nicole. "Will you meet me in front of the school tomorrow?"

"Okay, see you then."

"Bye," said Nicole. She hung up the phone. She pulled her algebra book out of her backpack and propped it up on her bed. She flipped through the pages and found her assignment. Unable to concentrate, she turned on the popular radio station, WKSG. She looked through her backpack, found a pencil and notebook, and began her work.

She finished four problems by the time the set of songs had ended. She then heard the booming voice of Danny Chavez, the DJ who dedicated songs over the radio:

"Well, hey, all you lovebirds out there. Now's the time to call in your requests for that special someone and let them know how very special they are, right over the radio."

Nicole began her fifth problem. She was just starting to add some fractions when the DJ's voice got her attention:

"This first request goes out to a very special lady from Eastbrook High. She may not know it, but she has a secret admirer."

This should be good, Nicole thought. *Probably another one of those football players that Cindy Jacobs likes to date.* The DJ's voice boomed though the radio: "If your name is Nicole Clayton from Eastbrook, you are the lucky girl."

Nicole dropped her pencil and screamed. *This must be a joke*, she thought. She picked up the radio and shook it, but the DJ's voice was real.

"Nicole, your secret admirer wants to tell you he has watched you from afar and he wants to dedicate this song to you." The DJ's voice left, and the slow beat of a love song came on.

14

Nicole was just starting to add some fractions when the DJ's voice got her attention.

Nicole put her face down into her pillow and screamed again. From outside the closed bedroom door, she heard her mom call.

"Is everything okay, Nicole?"

"Yeah, Mom," said Nicole, lifting her head out of the pillow. She felt like throwing up.

"Okay. 'Night, sweetie."

Nicole buried her head back in the pillow again. *Is this someone's idea of a joke?* she wondered.

The phone rang and she looked over at it. *Probably the joker himself, calling to see if I really believed it.* She reached for the cord and pulled it out of the wall, silencing the phone. She put on her pajamas and turned off the light. Nicole pulled the covers over her head and tried to fall asleep.

Chapter 3

Nicole jumped out of the bus and onto the sidewalk. She ran over to her usual meeting place, but Grace wasn't there yet. Nicole looked at her watch. *Hurry up, Grace.*

As she stood by the front steps, a group of girls walked past, staring at her. She heard one of them whisper, "Is that her?" Nicole tried to hide her face in her turtleneck sweater and looked at the ground. A voice behind her made her jump.

"Hey, what's going on?"

Nicole turned to see Grace grinning behind her. "Grace," said Nicole. "You scared me half to death."

"Why?" Grace stared at her.

"What's the matter?"

"You mean you haven't heard?"

"Heard what?" Grace asked.

Nicole took a deep breath. "Someone dedicated a song to me on WKSG last night," she said.

Grace's eyes widened. "Who?" Grace sat on the steps, pulling Nicole down beside her.

"I don't know," Nicole said. "The DJ said I had a secret admirer, but I think it was a joke."

"No way! A secret admirer? I bet it's not a joke." Grace looked around at all the passing students, as if any of them could be the one.

"Yeah, right," said Nicole. "Who would admire me?" Nicole looked up and saw Toby looking down at her. The sunlight shined like a halo around his head. She blocked the sunlight from her eyes with the palm of her hand.

"Hey, Nicole," said Toby.

"Um, hi, Toby," said Nicole.

He stood smiling down at her.

Nicole swallowed. She could see Grace grinning.

"You look nice today," said Toby.

"Thanks." Nicole brushed some dust from the stone steps.

Toby cleared his throat. "Well, I guess I'll see you in biology class." He waved good-bye.

As soon as Toby was far enough away not to hear, Grace turned to Nicole. "Oh my gosh! It's Toby!" she shouted.

"I don't think so," said Nicole.

Grace looked around to see if anyone was listening. "Tell me exactly what the dedication said," she whispered.

Nicole groaned. She didn't want to tell Grace anything else, but she knew she had to tell her. "The DJ said that the admirer has been watching me from afar," said Nicole.

Grace squealed. "Hello in there." She knocked on Nicole's head, as if to see if anyone was home. "It said, 'he's been watching you from afar.' Think. Everyone at school has seen Toby spying on you." Grace seemed very pleased with herself.

"He does not spy on me," Nicole said.

"Excuse me, but last week I was sitting next to him in geometry class. He was writing your name all over his notes," Grace said. "His face got really red when he saw me looking."

Nicole swallowed. The bell rang.

"Just a coincidence," said Nicole. She stood up and brushed dirt off her pants.

"We'll just have to see about this," said Grace.

Chapter 4

Nicole kicked at the dirt on her way to work that afternoon. It seemed like everyone at school had been looking and pointing at her all day.

Some girls even came up and asked her who the admirer was—but it didn't seem like they were making fun of her. One of her teachers even mentioned it in class, which made Nicole's face turn red. One boy in her algebra class even accused her of making the dedication herself, but she could tell he was only teasing.

She began to wonder if it were possible. *Do I actually have a secret admirer? Could it really be Toby?*

The bell jingled as she entered the

pet store. Sam sat behind the counter, dusting the cash register. He looked up when she came in. "Hey, Nicole," he smiled.

"Hi, Sam." She walked over to the counter and put her stuff down.

Sam smiled. "So, I hear you're a celebrity," he said.

"Oh no," said Nicole. "You heard, too?"

Sam raised his eyebrows at her. "What's wrong?" he asked. "Isn't it fun to have a little attention?"

"I guess so." She bit her lip. "I'm just not used to people even knowing my name, let alone details about my love life," she said.

Sam smiled again. "Love life, huh?" he said. "So who *is* this new guy in your life?"

Nicole blushed. "That's not what I meant," she said. "I don't even have a love life. I have no idea who it is."

"You really don't have a clue?"

asked Sam.

"To be perfectly honest, up until this afternoon I thought it was all a joke," said Nicole.

"You thought it was a joke?" Sam leaned toward her.

"Well, yeah. I'm not exactly the type of girl who gets many radio dedications," said Nicole. "That kind of thing only happens to girls like Cindy Jacobs."

"Not every guy is in love with Cindy Jacobs," he said.

"Well, if you find one who isn't, send him my way," said Nicole. "Anyway, I better get to work before I lose my job."

Sam threw her a work apron and walked toward the animal cages. "Which do you prefer?" he asked. "Bird poop or puppy poop?"

Nicole smiled. "I'll guess I'll take puppy poop," she said.

Sam laughed. "All right then,

march!" He tried to keep a serious face, but he couldn't help smiling.

"Okay, okay. I'm marching," she said. Nicole went toward the puppy cages, and Sam walked toward the birds.

She began cleaning the cage, which was not nearly as disgusting as she'd thought it would be. The room was quiet. She called over to Sam, "So what kind of stuff do you like to do when you're not cleaning up after animals?"

Sam glanced up from a box of bird food. "This *is* what I like to do," he said. "It used to be a hobby, but I turned professional."

Nicole stood up. "Your father must be so proud," she joked.

"And a little jealous," he joked back at her.

Chapter 5

The next week of school was a nightmare for Nicole. Everywhere she went, people pointed and stared at her. Strangers asked her if she had found out the name of her secret admirer. It seemed like every person at school knew her name and the story of her radio dedication. To make matters worse, no matter where Nicole went, she found Toby lurking around.

The only fun she had the past week was at work, where she and Sam became better friends each day. It was good to have a place where she didn't have to worry about radio dedications and gossip.

Exactly one week after the first

dedication, her admirer sent another message over the radio. Nicole sat in the kitchen working on her algebra homework. She suddenly heard her name from the radio in her sister's bedroom:

"Hey, Nicole Clayton of Eastbrook High, do you remember your secret admirer?" Nicole heard her little sister, Melinda, squeal.

"Nicole, Nicole! Quick! It's him again." Nicole ran into Melinda's room and sat down on the bed next to her sister. Her mom stood in the doorway to listen:

"Well, he wants you to know that he is still around, waiting for the perfect moment to tell you his name. He also wants to tell everyone out there listening what an incredible girl you are, Nicole. This song's for you."

A guitar played a few chords and then the singer began:

"From the moment I saw you there,

On the steps with sunlight in your hair
. . ."

Nicole jumped up off the bed and turned off the radio before the singer could sing another line. She couldn't believe that this was actually happening again. Nicole saw a worried look on her mom's face.

"I don't know about this, sweetie," her mom said. "What if this boy is dangerous?"

Nicole's mom looked even more worried. "Has anyone been bothering you at school, honey?" she asked. Nicole could feel her face turn red. *I can't believe this is happening to me. I'm actually sitting here discussing my secret admirer with my mother*, she thought.

"No, Mom," she said. "A little teasing is all. People are curious."

Her mom looked worried. "Do you have any idea who he is?" she asked.

"No. I still think it may be a joke or something," said Nicole.

Melinda said, "I think it's romantic."

"You would," said Nicole, messing up her sister's hair.

"I wish someone would dedicate a song to me," said Melinda. She fell down on her bed and looked up at the ceiling.

Nicole rolled her eyes, but her mom just laughed. "Don't you think you're a little young for boys?" she asked. Nicole was glad to see her mom in a happier mood and not talking about the secret admirer.

"You're never too young to dream," said Melinda. She closed her eyes and smiled in her romantic dream.

"Okay, enough of that, young lady," said Nicole's mom. "It's time for everyone to get to bed."

Twenty minutes later, when her teeth were brushed and her face was washed, Nicole lay in bed staring at the ceiling. *This wondering is driving me crazy. Who could it be?* She started thinking about every boy in every class she had. She counted them like sheep until she fell asleep.

"Can you believe it?" Nicole said into the phone the next morning. She waited for her toast to pop up as she spoke. "Another song. This is embarrassing."

"But I love that song," Grace told her. "It's just so romantic."

"Well, I think it's just embarrassing."

"From the minute I saw you sitting there," Grace began to sing off key, "on the steps with sunlight in your hair."

"Will you just shut up?" Nicole said. "You're no help at all."

"No help?" Grace sputtered. "I've narrowed your secret admirer down to a few possible suspects. Just meet me on the front steps before school."

Chapter 6

As Nicole got off the bus and walked to their meeting place, she saw Grace. She was on the steps looking through a large green book. As Nicole got closer, she saw that it was last year's yearbook.

"Hey," Nicole said. She sat down next to Grace.

"Hey," said Grace. She didn't look up from the yearbook on her lap. There were red circles drawn around half the boys on the page. Grace continued to look at the page. She then circled another face.

"That's your plan?" Nicole asked. "The yearbook?"

"I've been working on it all night."

*As Nicole got off the bus and walked to their
meeting place, she saw Grace.*

Nicole reached over and flipped through a few pages. Most of the boys' pictures were circled in red. "I thought you narrowed it down to just a few suspects," Nicole groaned.

"I have," Grace said. "I cut out the whole chess team and most of the math club."

Nicole looked at the circled faces. Her eyes stopped at the first one. "Jared Christensen? Are you nuts?"

Grace looked at her, wide-eyed. "Why?" she asked.

"He's a senior. He wouldn't notice me even if I went and sat on his lap at lunch today," said Nicole.

Grace's face brightened. "Would you really do that?"

"It was a joke," said Nicole. She shook her head in disbelief.

Grace raised her eyebrows. "I was just wondering."

"Okay, who else have you got?" asked Nicole, examining the book.

"Tom Woods? Oh, you don't really think it could be him, do you?" Her eyes opened wide. "He's so strange."

Grace nodded and patted Nicole's back. "It's a sad thought, but yes."

Nicole flipped through a few more pages, and Grace began to sing again. "From the minute I saw you sitting there . . ."

Nicole turned a page and saw Toby's circled face looking up at her.

Grace kept singing, "On the steps with sunlight in your hair . . ."

"Oh, my gosh, that's it!" Nicole shouted. "The words! The song!"

"Sure, they're corny. But that doesn't mean he's a weirdo or anything," said Grace.

"No, Grace, the words are a clue. Don't you get it? 'From the minute I saw you sitting there on the steps,'" Nicole said. "Don't you see?"

"See what?"

"It has to be Toby," Nicole said. "I

was sitting on the steps when he talked to me."

Sam wasn't there when Nicole got to work that afternoon. Mr. Johnson came out from the storeroom just as she was tying her apron strings into a bow.

"Nicole," said Mr. Johnson with a smile.

"Hey, Mr. Johnson," said Nicole.

"You sound just like Sam the way you say that," he said. He winked at her. "He's a good kid."

"Yes, he is," said Nicole.

"He'll be back shortly," Mr. Johnson told her. "He had some errands to run." He pushed his glasses higher on his nose. "I have to go to the post office to pick up a package. Do you mind watching the store for a few minutes?"

"I think I'll be okay," said Nicole. She grabbed a rag and began to wipe down the counter. She scrubbed a wad of gum stuck to the front of the register.

Mr. Johnson took off his apron and grabbed his coat. He stood in front of the door. He looked worried. This was Nicole's first time alone in the store. "Sam should be in soon, but I won't be long, either."

Nicole smiled. "I'll be fine, Mr. Johnson. Don't worry."

He nodded and ran out the door. "I'll be back soon," he said. The door jingled as it closed behind him.

Nicole spent time cleaning out all the animal cages. She looked at the clock every few minutes. *I wonder where Sam is*, she thought.

When everything was cleaned and polished and all the food refilled, she went behind the counter and pulled up a stool. She sat and wondered what to do. She reached into her backpack and pulled out the yearbook.

Opening the book, she turned to the page that had Toby's picture on it. He smiled at her with a goofy grin.

"It can't be him. It just can't," she said out loud.

"Can't be who?"

She turned and saw Sam smiling over her shoulder. She slammed the yearbook shut. "Oh, nothing," she said. "I didn't realize I was talking out loud."

She glanced toward the back of the store and saw the storeroom door was open. *He must have come in the back way*, she thought. "Where have you been?" she asked. "Mr. Johnson said you'd be gone only a few minutes."

Sam shifted his weight. "I was just out running errands."

"Oh." She knelt down to put the book in her backpack, but Sam grabbed it out of her hands.

He swung the book in front of her, teasing her. "So, what's all this about?"

Nicole tried to remain calm. "Nothing, just a project Grace and I are working on," she said.

"A project?" he said. Sam began

looking through the yearbook.

Nicole jumped at him. "Stop it," she said. "Give that back." She grabbed the book and walked toward the door.

"Nicole, stop." Sam grabbed her by the shoulders. His face was pale. "I'm so sorry."

She only shrugged, but she could tell he meant it.

"I didn't mean to upset you," he said.

Nicole sighed. "No, I'm sorry," she said. "I shouldn't have been so secretive. It's just that . . . I feel stupid, I guess."

"I don't think you're stupid," he said. They sat down on two stools behind the counter.

Nicole took a breath. "Grace and I were going through the yearbook trying to figure out who this secret admirer is from the radio."

Sam smiled. "You're that curious?"

"I just figured the sooner I find out who he is, the sooner people will stop whispering about me at school," she said.

"Maybe I can help," he said.

Nicole stared at him. "Help?"

"Yeah," he said. "If you're trying to discover a mystery man, who better to help you than a man?" He flexed his muscles.

Nicole laughed.

"I could get information from your suspects much easier than you," he said.

"Why would you want to do that for me?" Nicole asked.

Sam leaned in closer to her. "Because we're friends, Nicole."

Her fingers picked at some chipping paint on the counter. "Well, thanks," she said.

"So, let's see the suspects." Sam clapped his hands together and reached for the yearbook.

Chapter 7

Two days later, Nicole, Grace, and Sam watched Toby from across the cafeteria. It wasn't hard to convince Grace to let Sam join their secret operation. Grace always loved the chance to meet new boys.

Still, Nicole couldn't help but feel like Grace was staring every time Nicole talked to Sam or laughed at one of his jokes. She would look over, and Grace would smile at her and give her the thumbs-up sign. It embarrassed Nicole.

Sam leaned in and placed his palms flat on the table. "Okay, should I do it?"

Nicole shook her head. "I don't

know," she said. "What if he's not the one? It would be so embarrassing if he thought that . . ."

Grace put her hand up to shush her. "Nicole, we've talked about this," she said.

Sam nodded. "He doesn't have to know you sent me," he said. "I'll act totally natural."

Nicole leaned forward to whisper. "How natural is it to walk up to someone you don't know and say, 'Hey, so are you Nicole's secret admirer?'"

Sam grinned. "Trust me, okay?"

Nicole's heart beat faster. "Well, okay," she said. "But remember, don't walk back here. We'll meet at the front steps in ten minutes, okay?"

Sam saluted her. "Okay, chief."

Nicole laughed. *He's always making jokes*, she thought.

Sam got up and walked straight to the table where Toby sat alone, reading.

Nicole and Grace stood up and walked the other way. They tried not to act suspicious.

Once they were outside the cafeteria, Grace exploded with excitement. "Sam really likes you, Nicole," she said.

Nicole sighed. "Don't be dumb. We're just friends." She sat down on the front steps of the school and stared at the side door of the cafeteria.

Grace sat down next to her. "You're *not* just friends," Grace grinned. "Do you see the way he looks at you?"

Nicole kept her eyes on the cafeteria door. "If he likes me so much, then why is he offering to help me find my secret admirer?"

"I don't know why," said Grace. "All I know is that whoever this secret admirer is, I can't imagine that he'd be better for you than Sam."

"What do you mean?" asked Nicole.

"In case you didn't notice, you two are perfect for each other," said Grace.

"You both like animals."

Nicole groaned. "That's just a coincidence."

Grace kept on. "You laugh at every word he says."

"Well that doesn't . . . Shhh! Here he comes," said Nicole. Across the grass, they saw Sam come out of the cafeteria door and walk straight toward them. They ran to meet him.

"What happened?" asked Grace. She tried to catch her breath as she spoke.

"Do you really want me to tell you?" Sam laughed to himself.

"Sam, please do not try to be funny right now," said Nicole.

"Okay, okay," said Sam. "It's not him." Nicole felt relieved.

"What did he say? How did you ask him?" asked Grace. Sam answered Grace's questions but looked at Nicole.

"I just told him I was your older brother and I was looking out for you," he said. "I asked him if he had any idea who your admirer was, and he said no."

"What if he was lying?" asked Grace.

"He wasn't. Trust me," said Sam. Again, he talked directly to Nicole.

Finally, Nicole spoke. "But, Sam, I don't even have an older brother."

"I know that, and you know that, but Toby doesn't," he said. He grinned. "He went on and on trying to get me to put in a good word for him. He isn't your radio admirer, but he sure does like you a whole lot."

Grace and Sam laughed.

"Cut it out. You can be sure that I don't feel the same way," said Nicole.

Chapter 8

Nicole, Grace, and Sam spent the next two weeks crossing people off their list of suspects. Nicole and Grace sat and watched while Sam approached guy after guy and asked him if he was Nicole's admirer. Each time, the guy said no.

With all the investigating they were doing, Nicole was spending a lot of time with Sam. The more time she spent with him, the more things she liked about him.

She began to think that maybe Grace was right. *Maybe I should forget about finding the secret admirer and just tell Sam how I feel*, she thought. It had been two weeks, and there was still no word from her secret admirer. Still, she didn't think she should just give up at this point, not after all their hard work.

At lunch, Nicole slid her tray down the cafeteria line. She looked at the metal dishes of food behind the glass.

"What'll you have, sweetie?" asked the cafeteria lady.

"Just some potatoes, please."

"There you go."

She waited in line to pay for her lunch and looked across the cafeteria. She looked at the table where she, Sam, and Grace met every day. They were waiting for her. She smiled.

"Hi, Nicole." She recognized the voice even before she turned.

"Hi, Toby."

He stood and smiled at her, holding a tray of meatloaf. "You're looking lovely today," he said.

"Thanks," she smiled. She felt more comfortable around him now that she knew he wasn't her secret admirer. She slid her tray up to the register.

"That'll be $1.25," said the lady at the cash register.

Nicole pulled her wallet out of her backpack and took out a five-dollar bill. She handed it to the lady.

Toby cleared his throat and leaned on the counter. "So how's that secret admirer of yours?" he asked. "Have you found out who he is?"

Nicole froze. She decided to play along with Sam's little lie. "Nope, but my brother and I are still looking," she said.

Toby raised his eyebrows. "Your brother?"

Nicole shifted her weight. "Yeah," she said. "He talked to you the other day."

"No, I don't remember," he said. "I didn't even know you had a brother."

Nicole's heart pounded. "Yeah," she said. She pointed over to the table. "That's him over there, sitting with

Grace."

Toby nodded, but looked confused. "Oh," he said. "Sam's your brother? Well, he talked to me, but he didn't tell me he was your brother."

Nicole suddenly felt very strange. "What did he say?" she asked.

"Well, he just asked me if I knew what our homework was for World History. We're in the same class. That's it." Toby took a step back, staring at her.

"He didn't ask about my admirer?" she asked.

"No, why would he?" asked Toby. "Nicole, are you okay?"

Nicole left her lunch tray on the counter and walked toward the table. "No," she mumbled. "No, I'm not."

Sam smiled as she got to the table. He pulled a chair up next to his and motioned for her to sit down. She remained standing.

"Hey, Nicole, have a seat," said

Sam.

She shook her head, glaring at him. "What is this, some kind of a joke?"

"Nicole, slow down," he said. He put his hands up in front of himself. "You're not making sense."

"You've been lying to me," said Nicole. Her voice rose. People at nearby tables turned to watch them.

His eyes grew wide. "What?"

"Nicole, what is this?" asked Grace.

Nicole answered Grace but kept her gaze focused on Sam. "He's been lying the entire time."

Grace sighed. "What?"

Nicole ignored her. "Toby told me you never asked him about the secret admirer," she said to Sam.

"I can explain," he said.

"You lied to me," she hissed.

Sam lowered his voice to try to get Nicole to lower hers. Everyone was watching them. "You don't under-stand," he whispered.

"I understand," she laughed. "It must have been hilarious watching the sad little nobody search for her long-lost love." She wiped a tear off her face with the back of her hand.

Sam stood up and walked toward her. "No, you don't understand."

"Just forget it," she said. She pushed past him and rushed out of the cafeteria.

Later that night, Nicole was lying facedown on her bed when she heard her bedroom door open. Soon, she felt the bed sink down as someone sat next to her. She heard Grace's voice.

"Nicole, what's going on?" she asked.

Nicole kept her face hidden in her pillow and covers. Her words were muffled, but she knew Grace would understand them. "I don't know," she said. "All I know is that he lied. He never asked Toby about the radio dedication."

"There may be a very good explanation for that," said Grace.

Nicole turned over and sat up, suddenly angry. "You're taking his side?" she demanded.

"No," said Grace. She folded her hands on her lap. "I just don't think you should jump to conclusions."

"Well, what did he say after I left?" asked Nicole. She picked some fuzz off the blanket.

Grace sighed. "He said it isn't what it sounds like, but he wouldn't tell me anything else."

"Oh, that's convenient," Nicole said. She laughed bitterly.

"He just said he needs to talk to you about this personally," said Grace.

"Well that's too bad because I don't want to talk to him," said Nicole. She folded her arms.

Grace tossed a pillow at her. "Don't be childish and ruin a great relationship just because of a misunderstanding."

50

"You don't lie to someone you have a great relationship with," said Nicole.

"What are you going to do about work?" asked Grace.

"I don't know," said Nicole. "I guess I'll just ignore him."

"That's a good solution," said Grace. She gave Nicole a strange look.

"Well, I can't quit," Nicole said. She brought her feet up on the bed and rested her chin on her knees. "My mom hasn't found a new job yet, and we need the money."

"Well, I hope that when you see him, you will come to your senses and talk to him," said Grace.

"That's not likely," mumbled Nicole.

Chapter 9

The next day, Grace waited for Nicole at her locker after class.

"This has been the worst day I've had since this whole mess started," said Nicole.

"Well, hello to you, too," said Grace. "What's the matter now?"

"Everyone has heard about my little scene in the cafeteria," said Nicole. She looked over her shoulder. Two girls walked by and sneered. "Now not only am I famous, but I'm famously mean," Nicole whispered.

"Nobody thinks you're mean," said Grace. She looked in Nicole's locker mirror and put on lipstick.

"Are you kidding? I practically

threw a fit."

"Have you seen him today?" Grace asked. She put the cap on her lipstick.

"No. Maybe his lies made him sick, and he had to stay home."

"That is really not a very nice thing to say," Grace said. She shut Nicole's locker and walked toward the front of the school.

Nicole followed her. Another pair of girls walked past, giggling. Nicole groaned. "I can't wait to get out of here."

"And go to work?" asked Grace.

"Don't remind me," said Nicole.

"You should just talk to him," said Grace. They walked out the front doors and into the sunshine.

"I'll call you when I get home, okay?" said Nicole.

As she walked to work, Nicole was prepared to ignore Sam. When she got there, she found only Mr. Johnson. He sat behind the counter with an adding machine and papers.

"Hello, Nicole," he said.

"Hey, Mr. Johnson." Nicole lifted herself onto the counter and took off her backpack.

"Have a nice day at school?" he asked.

"It was okay," she said. She scratched at something stuck on her jeans.

"Just okay?" he said. He bent low so she would look at him.

"Well, I guess I've been having some social problems lately," she said.

"Oh, I'm sorry," he said. "I'm surprised that anyone would give a sweet girl like you any trouble."

"It's not that anyone's giving me trouble," she said. She hesitated, then said, "It's just that I never seem to fit in anywhere."

Mr. Johnson gave her a knowing smile. "I think things will get better with time, my dear."

Nicole glanced around the shop. *Where is Sam?* she wondered. She cleared her throat. "So, is it just us today?" she asked.

"Well, Sam's not coming in, if that's what you mean," said Mr. Johnson. He winked.

Nicole felt her face get red. "Oh, I don't care. I was just . . ."

"He said he had a problem to deal with," said Mr. Johnson. He unplugged his adding machine. "Anyhow, I'll be in the back unloading some supplies if you need me. I think you'll have plenty of work to keep yourself busy." He grabbed his things and started toward the back of the shop.

"Okay," said Nicole. She jumped off the counter and grabbed her apron.

"Oh, by the way," he said. He turned back to Nicole. "I signed up for an advertisement on WKSG. Will you listen and yell back to me when you hear it?"

"No problem, I'll listen," said Nicole. She walked over to the radio on the counter and turned it on. It was already set to the station as Mr. Johnson disappeared into the back room.

The sound of popular music filled the room as Nicole worked. *Kind of a strange station for Mr. Johnson to advertise on,* she thought. *How many teenagers need to come to the pet store?*

Nicole tapped her foot to the music as she cleaned out the birdcages. She was just putting the food away in the supply cabinet when she heard the voice of the DJ. "Remember, you get all the new music you want on WKSG."

Nicole moaned. She imitated the DJ's voice. "Yeah, and you also get all the heartache and popularity you *don't* want on WKSG." She shook her head and closed the supply closet.

The DJ continued to talk. "We all know that WKSG dedications are usually done at night, but today we are going to make an exception for a very special listener that we all remember."

"Oh no! Not again," said Nicole.

"Hey Nicole Clayton, I know you have been having a hard time, and so does your secret admirer. He wants to give you something to make you feel better. Go open the door to the pet shop where you work right now."

Nicole walked to the door. She felt as if someone was watching her. The DJ's words faded away. She heard only her own heartbeat as she reached for the doorknob. She opened the door and saw nothing. "Very funny. What will they think of next?" she said.

Then she heard a whimper. She looked down and saw a puppy with a red bow tied around its neck. A note was tied to the bow.

She picked up the puppy. It was warm and soft in her arms. It licked her nose and she giggled. She took a

Nicole picked up the puppy. It was warm and soft in her arms.

deep breath and unfolded the note. It said: "Please go back inside,

Your Secret Admirer."

She turned, went back in the door, and placed her puppy in the cage with the others. Sam stood in front of the counter, his hands in his pockets.

"Hey," he said.

"I don't understand," she said.

"Nicole, I did lie to you, and I'm sorry," he said. "But I only lied because I wanted to get to know you. I figured helping you find your secret admirer was a great way." He paused. "The truth is, *I* dedicated those songs to you on the radio."

"You?" she asked with surprise.

Sam nodded. "I saw you at school a few months before you got the job here. When we finally met, I knew you were special and . . ."

Nicole ran and hugged him. She felt his heart pounding. He was as nervous as she was.

"Sorry I wouldn't listen to you when you tried to explain," she said. She stepped back and looked at him.

"I never should have lied in the first place," he said. "It was a stupid way to get your attention."

Nicole smiled. "Well, I guess I can forgive that," she said. "But if we're going to hang out, we have got to do something about your taste in music."

He gasped. "What?" He grabbed his chest, as if her insult had pierced his heart.

Nicole laughed. "Come on, those songs you dedicated were really corny," she teased.

Sam looked into her eyes. "Well, they worked, didn't they?" He held out his hand, just like he had on Nicole's first day in the shop.

This time she took it, smiling. "Yeah, I guess they did."